The Sky, My Fish Pond

A novel by

Maziar Saffariantoosi

1

Chapter One
A teardrop in the pond.. 4

Chapter two
Insomnia 8

Chapter Three
The guilt 13

Chapter four
 Fish tears 15

Chapter five
The cat 22

Chapter six
Prisoners 24

Chapter seven
Mr. Crow 38

Chapter eight
 The abyss 44

Chapter nine
The sky 47

Chapter ten
The end of the story from another point of view 49

About The Auther...55

Chapter One
A teardrop in the pond

The front door opened with a creak, announcing Tohru's mother entrance. Tohru ran to the door and followed his mother's shadow on the ground till he reached her and threw himself in her arms. Tohru pulled off a chunk of bread that his mother had bought and said, "I'm taking it for the fish". His mother nodded with a cold look.

Tohru ran happily to the pond which was in the middle of the yard. The pond with its small square turquoise tiles was flashing to him. He would always sit at the edge of the pond and throw rice or chunks of bread for the fish. He had bought these fish some time ago and his only hobby was spending time with them. There was always a small plastic bag with breadcrumbs in his pants pocket. He thought to himself that he had no other choice left. His mother never played with him.

She did not even have the patience to tolerate what he did. Only a cold pitiful look was the fixed expression on his mother's face. Maybe it was because she was working so hard. Tohru did not have a father, but he did not know exactly why. No one had told him. He did not know whether his father had left them or had joined his grandfather in a frame with a black ribbon. Maybe he had gone on a long journey that he was returning from these days. Tohru always thought he must be very much like his father. Maybe his father looked just like Tohru, but taller with a beard and mustache. The absence of his father had withered his mom a lot. She used to be kinder, but day after day, she was becoming more languid and irritable than before. Tohru explained all these to the fish, pondering, "I wish the fish would talk to me and tell me about their concerns."

He looked at the fish pond thinking, "I wonder if these fish have any problems. They never worry about food and no danger threatens them in the pond. Of course the pond is a small place, but it is safer than the sea. You can't have your cake and eat it too. Freedom is dangerous for fish."

4

Tohru was deep in these thoughts when his mother called out to him, "Tohruuuuuu, Tohruuuuuu, lunch is ready!"

Tohru was distracted for a moment by a smell. That of a delicious meal. But the smell was not coming from their own house. For a long time, her mother's food did not taste good. In fact, she did not seem to enjoy eating at all, she only ate to satisfy her hunger. But this smell was different. The smell of delicious food, maybe Soba Noodles or something else. The smell was from a neighbor's house. The house where a boy named Yoshiro lived.

Tohru had never seen Yoshiro, but he was always jealous of him at heart. How can someone be jealous of a person whose face he has never seen? Well, Yoshiro also used to ride his tricycle in the yard. It could be heard, but Tohru's mother had broken his tricycle. Tohru could not remember why. Maybe he had driven her crazy once. His mother would lose her temper easily.

There was another thing too. Yoshiro's mother always called him nicely, saying, "Yoshiro … dear … my dear son, lunch is ready. Wash your hands and come to mommy…."Tohru's mother had never called him that way. Not even once had she told him my darling or even my son...

Tohru fell deep into his thoughts for a moment. His mother's scream echoed in his ear. He realized the bitter truth. His mother never loved him. There was no motherly feeling. It was just coercion. A tear slid down Tohru's cheek and hung down his chin. After little resistance and sway, it dropped off into the water.

Chapter two
Insomnia

It was midnight. Tohru could not sleep. Maybe it was the news he had heard that was to blame. Lack of drinking water was rampant. The news anchor had repeatedly stated that the water crisis was serious. He could hear his mother snoring and puffing. Suddenly he heard another noise, the splash of water. There might be something in the water. Tohru tiptoed to the door. He opened it slowly and saw a scene that stunned him. The fish were coming out of water. They fluttered their small fins to fly. Their red wings were shining in the moonlight. And Tohru was just looking at them, mesmerized by the scene without screaming or showing any signs of being scared. The gold fish bigger than the others moved its tail slowly and started coming towards him, but Tohru did not feel the need to run away. The flying fish was not that bad, "Thank goodness sharks don't fly, nor do scorpions." Tohru was thinking when he saw the fish floating in the air just two steps away from him.

The fish was waving its fins and standing like a stationary helicopter. He shook his lips gently," Hello Tohru. ..."

Tohru was taken aback. The flying fish was strange enough, but the talking flying fish was extraordinary.

The fish repeated in a thick voice, "Hello ..."

"Hello, are you okay?" stuttered Tohru.

"Not bad," replied the fish.

"How do you know my name?" asked Tohru, "How come you started flying all of a sudden?"

-" When a drop of tear fell into the water, we felt some part of your memories and we wondered what had happened; but the curse was broken and we were able to get out of the water slowly."

-"Curse? Which curse?"

- "It's a long story."

- "I am curious to know."

-" Well, in principle, we the fish do not belong to water or sea at all."

-"Where do you come from then?"

-"The sky."

-" Can you explain more?"

- "My pleasure. Years ago, even before there were any humans, we used to travel in galaxies and went to different planets. Wherever we went, our bodies adapted themselves to the environment. If it was very cold, our bodies would grow wool and hair; and if it was hot, they would keep cold till we reached the Earth. The planet was full of water, just like a small blue plastic ball. We approached it and found it interesting to live in water for a while.

Tohru said in amazement, "You mean you have never wanted to get out of water since then?"

"Do not interrupt me," said the fish. "The point is that we had been being imprisoned here all the time. We could not get out of water till you shed that tear in it."
could not get out of water till you shed that tear in it."

Suddenly a fish with golden fins shouted that the sun was coming and that she could not feel her fins. Meanwhile, Tohru could hear the screams of other fish moaning all together. "Into water, immediately," the big fish cried. He himself dived into water at once. One by one, the fish jumped in. A small fish fallen behind with its mother pushed itself towards the edge of the

9

pond but collapsed before reaching the water. The magic was gone. The little fish's mother had fallen a few steps behind on the ground. The little fish was crying by the pond and tried to get to the water. Tohru rushed to the baby fish and threw it into the water. The fish in Tohru's hand shouted, "No, go to my mother, goooo." As he turned his head, he saw the mother fish. He ran towards her, but the orange cat reached earlier. The cat took the fish with its teeth.

The fish cried for help. Tohru ran towards the cat, but the cat pressed its teeth harder against the fish flesh, ran quickly away, and jumped onto the wall.

Tohru shouted, "Let her go, you asshole!" and when he was disappointed, he fell on his knees. The baby fish, watching everything from the water, opened and closed its mouth with sadness. None of his words could be heard by Tohru, only consecutive bubbles came onto the water and burst one after another. Tohru sat on the edge of the pond and shouted, "I'm sorry ... it was not my fault, I'm sorry... ."

The baby fish was looking at Tohru with deep hatred. The other fish came around the small fish and took him to the other side. The big fish looked at Tohru in despair. Tohru burst into tears. His tears fell into the water.

Suddenly Tohru's mother leaned out of the window and shouted, "What's with all the noise? Are you talking to yourself?"

"The cat took my fish," said Tohru sadly.
His mother shouted, "The hell with them all. I wish you would grow up. Go inside and get changed; you're wet all over."

Chapter Three
The guilt

Tohru was preoccupied all day. He could not forget the little fish's mother at all. He put the blame on himself. Other thoughts occupied his mind as well. The story told by the big fish was still incomplete. Tohru was curious as to what made the fish, who could adapt to any environment, live in water but no longer survive out of it. Could his tears have an effect tonight? And would he be able to talk to the fish anymore? Feeling anxious, Tohru turned on the TV so that it might perhaps help make him forget some of his concerns. But the news was also depressing, constantly mentioning terrorist attacks and water shortage tragedy. Whenever Tohru thought about lack of water, his throat would dry out and the thought that one day there would not be enough water disturbed him. He knew that the seas were full of water, but too salty to be used. A lot of problems could be solved if only they could eliminate the salinity of the water. But he did not know why the sea water was salty.

He changed the channel to a children's program. When his mother was home, she would not let Tohru watch children's programs. His mother kept repeating that he had grown up and should not watch children's programs or act childishly. But now that his mother was gone, he was fully entertained by the cartoons so long till there was one about a small lonely fish. Tohru drowned in his thoughts again... .

Chapter four
Fish tears

It was night. Tohru's mother was asleep. She would always work very hard and at night, her snores filled the house. Tohru went slowly near the pond and sat on the edge of the pond. He waited for the fish to come out. All he thought about was what if this time his magic did not work and the fish were not be able to come out anymore. But his worries did not last long. The fish came out of water one after another. The big fish was the first and then the fish with golden-fins and the other fish followed in a row. Tohru guessed this was a precaution as to dive into the water in case the magic disappeared after the sunrise.

The big fish turned to Tohru and said, "There is a

strange force in you. It is as if these tears have an effect every time."

"I am glad to see you again. I am sorry for your loss," said Tohru. "There was nothing we could do," the big fish said. "If you like, you can offer your condolences to the baby fish."

The baby fish was floating corner of the pond. The big fish said to the baby fish, "Weep outside of the pond. You'll make the water salty... ."

The little fish came out of the water. He looked at Tohru indifferently and went to a corner a short distance from the pond and started crying.

Tohru asked the big fish in surprise, "What did you mean that water becomes salty?"

The big fish asked, "Have you ever had a tear streaming down your cheek to your mouth and tasted it?"

Tohru remembered the first time his mother threw his toys away. He was very upset at that time. Her mother kept telling him that he had grown up. Tohru complained that he did not want to grow up, but his mother did not really listen to him.

Tohru recalled the tears he shed there, each sliding gently alongside his nose and sinking on his lips. He remembered exactly that taste.

Tohru said, "Yes, I remember it tasted salty. It was like salt."

"Well, if a large number of your tears fall down into this small pond; they make it salty just as the tears of this baby fish do," mentioned the big fish.

"I did not know fish cry too." said Tohru.

The big fish then explained, "No one sees the tears of the fish in water, but the fish cry even more than human beings. That is why their souls are purer. Why do you think the seawater is so salty then?!"

Tohru was overwhelmed. He hadn't known the reason for the salinity of the sea water all this time. But now he understood. The water crisis was just because the fish were trapped in water.

The big fish continued, "Although the effect of the fish tears is temporary, since a lot of fish cry constantly, the seawater has become salty. But the fish don't usually cry in rivers."

"But the sea is much bigger, how come they don't get as depressed in rivers?" asked Tohru.

"Yes, but it is still. With all its greatness it is not that different from a pond. It is just a bigger prison. The secret of the river is in its flow." answered the big fish.

"But it also eventually disgorges into a sea. So what is

there to enjoy in river?" asked Tohru curiously.

-"The route itself is important, not the destination. It is important to move and flow. Do not just seek the destination."

- "But not having a goal is awful."

-"Goal is different from destination. The goal is the path itself. The goal is to move forward. When you reach your destination and stay there, it is the beginning of your imprisonment and depression. That is why the fish reaching the sea, finally get tired after few years swimming."

Tohru did not understand what the fish was saying, but he nodded so that no one would think he was ignorant.

Tohru changed the subject, "By the way, tell me the rest of your story."

"Our destiny has a long story," said the big fish. "It may remain incomplete tonight. Isn't it better to go and comfort the baby fish in this remaining short time till morning?"

Tohru answered, "He hates me. He blames me for his mother's death."

- "So go and prove to him that it is not so; otherwise, both of you will live with this thought all through your lives."

Tohru walked slowly towards the baby fish.

He turned to him and said," No one was to blame for what happened last night."

The baby fish told Tohru with a sharp look, "No, I know very well who was to blame … ."

Tohru noted, "But I did my best. I saw you first and then your mother...."

-" No, I do not mean you at all. I was to blame… ."

- "What are you saying that, you could not do anything? The whole time I was trying to rescue you, you were calling your mother's name and telling me to save her."

-"You know why my mother fell behind me? She had always been one of the fastest fish. Because she threw me towards the pool with her tail and she went off course and fell on the ground."

The baby fish cried his eyes out. He turned to Tohru and said, "Thank you for rescuing me. You did what my mother wanted. It was not your fault, but now leave me alone."

Tohru wanted to say something to calm him down, but any word could make things worse. So he headed towards the big fish.

Tohru said, "Thank you for telling me to talk to him. Now

I am relieved. But can you tell the rest of your story?"
-"If it'll be left incomplete, then it's your fault," replied the big fish.

Tohru stared at the big fish in his eagerness.
The big fish continued, "We have been trapped on earth since a long time ago. I myself have been imprisoned for millions of years."
"How old are you?" asked Tohru.
-"I do not know exactly, but I have also experienced freedom hundreds of times more than what I have spent here. And I have seen many places."
-"I had no idea the fish would live that long. I wish I lived that long."
-"You do live as long, even longer than us, but rather in different forms. You are too a prisoner now. But it will be your turn to be released one day. By the way, how old are you?"

Tohru pondered. In fact, he could not remember when his last birthday was. There was no birthday party or talk about how old he was. He just knew he had grown up. His mother frequently reminded him of that. He could, however, remember Yoshiro's birthday party. Tohru thought to himself that maybe he was the same age as him.

Tohru looked into the fish's eyes and replied, "I am about six years old."

The fish said," So your whole life doesn't even count as a second of my life .Time passes quickly, but not for captive."

Tohru asked, "So what happened? Why have you been captured? Come on!"

But it was too late. The sun was rising. The little fish jumped into the water in the blink of an eye. The other fish jumped down into the water from different heights and a huge amount of water splashed on Tohru's head and face.

-"Did you wet yourself once again?"

Tohru turned his head and found his mother watching him in bewilderment.

Chapter five
The cat

Tohru attempted to weep for several days, but met with no success. He sat by the water and pushed himself to cry, but could not. There were no tears. It was as if his eyes had dried out. The fish were staring at him too. They had enjoyed freedom after ages. For many of them it was the first hand experience and consequently it was naturally painful for them to stay in the pond again. Tohru sometimes even sat next to it and peeled onions. And he shed tears in the water, but in vain. This magic only required real tears, not fake ones.

On the other hand, Tohru's curiosity was being aroused. He wanted to know the story and fate of the fish as soon as possible. Maybe he could help them. In this way, not only would the fish be free and happy, but also the water crisis would disappear for a long time.

Suddenly Tohru heard the cat meow. He went to the door and looked. It was the orange cat that had eaten the baby fish's mother. The cat immersing his paws in the water was trying to catch the fish. Tohru quickly ran to the cat and grabbed it. The cat limped and resisted. He injured Tohru's arm and elbow with his nails. Tohru felt a pain and burn but did not release the cat. He held the cat firmly with both hands. The cat hit Tohru hard on the forearm again. Tohru gripped the cat by the head and immersed it into the pond. The cat thrashed about but it was of no use. Tohru's blood drops slowly fell into the water and disappeared one by one. After a while, the cat did not move anymore. Tohru cried and tears fell one after another down into the water. Suddenly, Tohru's mother opened the front door and entered. As she was shocked by the scene, the fruits she had bought dropped to the ground. She ran towards Tohru.

Chapter six
Prisoners

Tohru's mother was very angry with him. When she realized Tohru had strangled the cat in the water with his hands, she was shaken up and her face went pale. She imprisoned Tohru in his room all during morning. Tohru's room had a very thin wooden door. Tohru could easily hear his mother talking to a man on the phone. His mother was constantly repeating a name which sounded like Mr. Crow. This name sounded a bit familiar to Tohru but did not make sense. Tohru was confused. He was thinking the whole time that it was almost midnight and the fish were coming out again. If Tohru had been a strong man, he could have easily broken this door, but he was just a little boy. Although he'd always felt the power of a man inside, it was useless this time.

Tohru looked down carefully. Damp had rotted the lower part of the door. Tohru rubbed the splinters gently with his hands and found that the other side of the door could be seen. He removed pieces enough to open a way and then he could tiptoe to the yard. The fish had not come out yet. Tohru sat on the edge of the pool waiting. All the fish gathered together up the water and slowly moved up one after another.

The golden-fins fish approached Tohru's elbow and asked," Does it still hurt?"

-" No, my mother disinfected it, but it still burns a little…,"replied Tohru.

The big fish came closer and said, "Thank you for saving our lives."

Tohru shook his head with a bitter smile. Tohru went on, "My mother imprisoned me for what I did, but I made good my escape tonight. I might not be as lucky the other nights. Please tell the rest of the story in no time."

"We had a good life here until we made friends with a genie who lived on water," said the big fish. In fact, he could stand on water. The genie had many other features and abilities. For example, he could transform himself into various forms, but after each change, his memory would reset and he would not remember anything from his previous life. Of course, it was as if he felt some part of his past in him."

-"So how does he remember to change again?" questioned Tohru.

-"The other genies reminded him, although he did not change during the time he was with us and he felt complete satisfaction with his condition; he talked to the fish every day; he was always jealous of our absolute freedom. You know that jealousy hurts the jealous himself more, and causes him not to see his own blessings and abilities, not to enjoy his life and to always seek happiness in other's lives. And it is like a fire that burns a person from within."

It reminded Tohru of himself and Yoshiro; how he had always been jealous of him, and this bothered him, yet another question occupied his mind. Wondering, he asked, "Couldn't he reshape as he wished? So why didn't he transform into a fish and fly with you to the other galaxies?"

-"Yes, but he could not abandon the earth and accept the dangers of freedom. You know, gaining freedom requires a certain amount of courage, even many sacrifices. Having more freedom requires more courage as many people who had the courage to gain freedom could not bear having it at all."

"I did not get this part, can you explain more?" stated Tohru.

The fish said, "Look, a canary has everything in a cage, food and a comfortable place to sleep. But if it wants to leave the cage, even if the door is open, it needs courage. The world outside that cage is full of dangers and wild birds. It may not even find anything to eat and also it no longer has the soft and comfortable place inside the cage. So it wavers between comfort and liberty....

Our story is the same, just like the Genie's. He always dreamed of our abilities, while if he wanted, he could have achieved them; but he showed little enthusiasm to accept the consequences.

Anyways, we got tired of your land after a while. We could not stay here any longer since this is our natural instinct to be in the flow. We said goodbye to the genie and informed him that we wanted to fly away the next day and leave. The genie begged us to stay and tell him more about our travels, but we had already made up our minds. We even offered him to accompany us, but he rejected it and instead cast a spell which then he threw into the water, and we've all been imprisoned like this.

So if we came out of water, we would die after a while as a direct consequence of the spell. The genie told us that it was only he could break the spell, not anyone else. He asked us to talk to him, but we were no longer interested in him; so he wove another spell and filled the water with predators such as sharks and carnivorous fish. We have always run away from these things.

It took a long time and lands appeared and then did the human. The genie was left off by the other genies because of his improper deeds. So he disguised himself as a human being and disappeared forever. He could not even remember he wanted to set us free, and that is why we've got stuck."

Suddenly the golden-fin fish said," Look, a cloud is covering the full moon. We can meet the wise old man."

Tohru asked in surprise, "Wise old man? Full moon?"

"The cloud in front of the full moon is the place where the wise old man lives. We used to talk to him before we were imprisoned and ask him our questions, but we have not seen him for ages." replied the big fish.

Tohru went on, "But when you were not imprisoned, there were no humans yet."

The big fish answered, "He is not a human being; he is a special and unique creature."

Tohru thought to himself," Of course he is; otherwise which human's house is located on a cloud?"

Tohru continued, "So what are you waiting for? Fly there and ask the old man how you can be released. Maybe he can help you find the genie. It is still the first night. You have a chance. There may not be another."

The big fish said, "He is right, but I cannot put your lives at risk. I need some volunteers to accompany me."

The golden-fin fish said, "I will." Five other fish also volunteered.

"I should come too. Your temporary release is due to my tears, maybe I can help," remarked Tohru.

The big fish said, "Well, maybe you are right. Hold our tails."

Tohru gripped the tails of the six fish firmly with his hand. At first, the tails were very slippery, but then he took them with both hands and was able to get used to it. The big fish told the other fish, "Stay close to the pond, we will be back."

And then it started to ascend with the other fish. The higher he went, the more fear and simultaneously freedom Tohru felt. When a cool breeze hit his face, he felt liberated. He had never looked at the stars or the moon from above this height. Suddenly one of Tohru's

28

hands slipped. Tohru shouted, "Help!"

The big fish said, "Be patient, we are almost there." Tohru's other hand was becoming loose when the fish reached the top of the cloud. Tohru could no longer hold the tails and shouted, but a little later he saw that he had fallen on something soft. He landed on a cloud, then turned his head and saw an old small hut.

"There it is …, the old man's house," said the golden-fin fish with great excitement.

Tohru went towards the hut with the fish. He opened the door and to his surprise, the inner view of the hut was like a palace; there was a very long corridor with gold pillars decorated with diamonds up to the end of the hall. Tohru looked at the hall floor in surprise. The entire floor was covered with thick smoke. Tohru could not even see his feet down his ankles. A little further on, they saw the old man on his throne puffing a cigarette, but the interesting thing was that instead of going up, the smoke went downwards and covered the floor. The number of cigarettes puffed did not seem to come to an end. The old man started in a scratchy voice, "Hello old friends and greetings to the cat killer … ."

"He did save our lives," said the golden-fins fish. "You should not call him a murderer … ."

The old man went on a grin, "He could have made the cat run away, but he did not and preferred to strangle the animal brutally. There is a lot of ferocity in it."

Tohru, flushed with anger and sadness, shouted, "He would have come back. And he definitely deserved it. He was the cat that orphaned the baby fish and ate his mother."

"So you did this to take revenge then. Have you not eaten fish yourself yet?" asked the old man.

Tohru yelled, "I have not had fish since I became friends with fish."

The old man wanted to answer Tohru, but the big fish interrupted him and said, "Please do not argue so much. We do not have much time. Please help us find that genie."

The old man grinned, "I do not think you need my help."

The golden-fin fish countered sharply, "How can we find him among all these people? We cannot completely free ourselves without his help."

"You have already found him, he is standing right behind you," mentioned the old man.

All the fish turned around.

The old man pointed his trembling fingers towards Tohru and said, "The jealous genie, the cat killer, Tohru the fish lover... ."

The old man laughed out loud and continued, "How could you not understand? Have you all forgotten that the genie said it was only he himself who could break the spell?"

The fish all looked at Tohru in surprise and hatred. Tohru himself was stunned too and was experiencing the worst feeling of his life ever. It was all his fault; the imprisonment of the fish, the death of the baby fish's mother, the water crisis.

The old man continued, "After living among the people for a while, he realized his ability and changed himself every now and then; of course every time he changed, it took him decades to gain his power, until he met the woman who is now his wife or better to say his mother...." Tohru was even more dumbfounded and sharpened his ears.

The old man added, "A housewife and a fisherman.... They seemed to have been having a good life, but unfortunately they did not have any children. After undergoing a lot of fertility treatments, they finally succeeded, but the child was a stillborn. Tohru's wife was depressed, so Tohru, who had realized his ability, transformed himself into a child to satisfy her, but after a while his wife wanted the same old husband, but she could not easily explain the story to Tohru."

Tohru thought a little. Suddenly it all made sense to him; his mother's coldness, the fact that he did not remember much of his past, that he had no birthday parties, that his mother imprisoned him at home, that she insisted he grow up faster, even his jealous spirit ... . One of the fish turned to Tohru and said, "It was all your fault. You bastard ... we must kill you ...!"

The whispers of a few more fish could be heard. Hateful voices grew louder. The big fish raised his voice and said, "It is better not to look for the guilty. Tohru is no longer the former genie. In fact, he is nothing like it. He wants to help us now...."

Then he turned to the old man and continued, "How can this spell be broken?"

The old man questioned, "Have you ever gone to the sea in the morning, Tohru?"

Tohru, who did not expect the old man to address him, thought for a while and remembered that he used to walk by the sea when he and his mother were happy.

Tohru said, "Yes, I used to go to the sea a lot. Our house is close to the sea. Sometimes I hear the sound of the waves if it is very quiet."

"If you look carefully, you will see that the sky meets the sea at the horizon and at the end of the sea. You will see that there is only one line between the blue sky and the sea," explained the old man.

Tohru imagined the sea in his mind and said, "You are right, looks like as if the sea and the sky merge into one another."

The old man said, " Well done. Exactly that point is the bridge between the sky and the sea where you can break the spell. You just have to go there and shed a tear. The sea effect is so enormous that all the fish in the ponds or lakes and rivers can fly again."

Tohru said, "How can I get to the end of the sea?"

The big fish replied with a question, "Didn't I tell you that one of your abilities is walking on water?"

"But I just forgot it," said Tohru.

"This is not something you might forget. It is in your nature. You just have to focus and have a desire for it," noted the big fish. Tohru turned to the old man and stared into his narrow eyes. The old man shook his head yes and said that the fish was right. The fish were all on cloud nine, both physically and emotionally.

Anyway, it was a happy atmosphere when the big fish countered, "Shake a leg, we don't have time, we have to reach the pond."

The moonlight dimmed over from the glass roof of the palace. The old man was fading slowly. He whispered, "Good luck!" at the last moment.

And then he completely disappeared. The golden-fin fish shouted at everyone to run to the door. The fish ran fast all towards the door.

The palace began to shake. The colored glass of the roof began to crack. The pillars broke one after another. Tohru dodged or jumped over them. The glass of the roof broke and dropped off. He saw all the fish at the door except the big fish who was coming behind him with blood dripping from his body. One splinter of the roof glass lodged into his body causing a deep wound.

The golden fin-fish cried, "Are you okay?"

"Doesn't matter. We have to hurry," the big fish replied in a low voice.

Tohru was shocked. He could not believe that he might lose the big fish. He was like his master, like a father, someone who was at his back all the time. The big fish threw Tohru down the cloud with his body. Tohru was approaching the ground in no time. While through the air, the big fish, along with the other fish, gathered around Tohru and turned their tails towards him so that

34

he could grab them. Then they slowed down to reach the ground.

As close as one or two meters to the ground, the intensity of the magic decreased and it was as if the fish were falling down. They made their way to the pond. The big fish fell into the water and splashed a big wave out of the pond. The other fish dived into the water one after another. The golden-fin fish hit the edge of the pond and was thrown to the middle of the yard. Tohru's leg also banged onto the edge of the pond and he fell to the side with severe pain and bloody leg. He closed his eyes in pain. Once he opened his eyes he saw the golden-fin fish was struggling in the middle of the yard. Tohru crawled towards him. He did not want the story of the baby fish mother to happen again.

Tohru reached for the golden-fin fish and grabbed it, the fish slipped once. He gripped it by the fin the second time. He was lifting it when suddenly a black beak caught the fish by its head. Tohru looked at him with fear. In front of him stood a tall black man with a few crow feathers on his head instead of hair. Apart from that, he was almost entirely bald and had a large beak instead of lips and mouth.

Tohru said, "Let him go ... I tell you let him go ... ."

Mr. Crow did not give up and pulled the fish more strongly. Suddenly the fins of the fish were torn off and Tohru lost his balance.

Tohru looked at his hand with tears in his eyes and saw a golden fin on the palm of his hand. He squeezed it and looked at Mr. Crow with anger.

His mother was standing next to the Mr. Crow, looking at Tohru worriedly.

Tohru shouted, "He ate my fish."

He jumped angrily at the Mr. Crow, but the man in black took him by the arms and pressed Tohru's arms so tightly that Tohru could not move.

Tohru looked at the Mr. Crow's face with hatred; his beak was coming close to Tohru's eyes.

Tohru turned and looked at his mother.

His mother said in a sad voice, "He is Mr. Crow. We've come to help you become the person you used to be."

Chapter seven
Mr. Crow

Tohru was sitting on a chair facing the dining table. The golden fin of the fish was pinned to his shirt as a sign of protest. His mother was standing two meters away from Tohru to take care of him. Mr. Crow sat on another chair facing Tohru. And he began to speak, "I know you are angry, but your mother and I have made an agreement. The fish will be my share and in return, I will help you change to the previous state. I have to tell you that in the past, you were...."

Tohru interrupted him and said, "I know everything myself, but I will not return to my previous state until I save the fish."

The Mr. Crow hit his hand on the table furiously and

continued, "But we have compromised. The fish should stay in the water and I should be allowed to catch them."

Tohru remarked, "What you have promised each other has nothing to do with me."

"It seems as if you have forgotten everything. The promise was actually between you and me," said Mr. Crow.

Tohru looked at Mr. Crow in astonishment and wondered, "What? Promise between me and you?"

"Yes, I'm a demon, just like you. I cast a spell on inside you because I did not have enough power to apply it to the whole sea and I wanted the fish to be mine. The sharks in the depths of the sea brought them up to the surface of water, and then it was my turn to eat. I really like the taste of fish; although it is not my main food, I prefer it."

Mr. Crow stuck out his tongue and licked around his beak and insidiously said, "They taste like your delicious golden-fin friend …."

Tohru got up to punch Mr. Crow, but Mr. Crow quickly threw Tohru back with his hand and pushed him on his chair.

He then continued, "Some time ago, something inside me warned me that the magic was broken somewhere, then I did some investigation and met your wife. She did not think like me, but we had common goals. Now we will make a new agreement based on which you will return to your previous state and then you will completely forget what has happened. In exchange, I will not eat the other lovely fish in your pond. Look at that woman in that corner. She loves you very much. She wants you to return to your former state...."

Tohru thought for a while and said, "I was a fisherman in my previous life, so if I change back, those fish will no longer matter to me. Besides, my goal is to save all the fish and provide people with drinking water."

Mr. Crow said, "Then we have serious problems with each other."

Then he put an ugly smile on his face. Tohru noticed the plastic bag full of bread crumbs in his pocket, the one with which he used to feed the fish. Then he grinned and said moaned, "Have you just realized that? We have had serious problems with each other since you swallowed my friend."

Mr. Crow's smile faded. Tohru took the bag of the bread crumbs out of his pocket and threw it at him. The bread grains irritated the Mr. Crow's eyes. Tohru quickly punched him and pushed the table towards him.

Mr. Crow collapsed and the table fell down on him. Tohru picked up a large colorless plastic bag from the corner of the kitchen quickly. His mother ran towards him but her foot slipped and she lost her balance. Tohru really wanted to help her. Contrary to Tohru's imagination, she had loved Tohru wholeheartedly all this time, but in a different way from what Tohru had expected. But now there was no time for this. It was a very critical situation. He jumped over his mother and went to the yard and then to the pool. He threw the bag into the water and the fish quickly rushed into it. Suddenly some familiar scenes flashed in front of his eyes. He was a fisherman. He used to throw nets into water and catch fish. The fish were moving inside the net. Tohru blinked a few times and those scenes disappeared from his sight. He quickly grabbed the bag that was full with all the fish and ran towards the door. His mother had forgotten to close the door in the yard. Tohru ran quickly and entered the alley. He had not stepped in the alley for a long time. He felt the sound and smell of the sea and ran through a number of alleys. He finally reached the beach. He ran quickly on the sand. It felt good, his feet on the warmth of the beach sand.

He could hear the screams of his mother and the

Mr.Crow from his back. Tohru became more anxious and ran faster. Mr.Crow ran very fast, but Tohru's mother was behind. Tohru fell down. He saw a piece of stone on the sand and threw it at Mr.Crow. The stone hit Mr. Crow's head and he collapsed. Tohru saw the bag of fish that had been punctured and was lying a few steps away. He quickly picked it up and reached the seashore. His mother's moans bothered him, but he tried to focus on his goal. When he reached the edge of the sea, he saw that water had poured out through that tiny hole and the fish could not reach the end of the sea with him, so he opened the bag and threw the fish into the sea one by one.

The baby fish who jumped last looked at Tohru and said quietly, "Thank you for everything."
The baby fish then jumped into the water. Tohru looked at the bottom of the bag and saw the big fish wounded and bloody. He was so busy and nervous that he had forgotten his wound.
Tohru held the fish gently in his hand and said, "No, you cannot die. I still need you. I have just been learning a lot from you."
He said this and tears welled up in his eyes.

The big fish smiled bitterly and said, "Keep your tears.

You need them at the end of the sea. I have experienced everything. Maybe dying for freedom is not so bad. A new experience ...."

Suddenly, a hand grabbed Tohru's arm. Tohru turned his head back. It was Mr. Crow standing in front of him with a bloody head and opening his beak to injure Tohru.

The big fish said, "I want to do something good for you and give you a last large meal to enjoy!" He then slipped from Tohru's hand and jumped into Mr. Crow's throat. The fish was so big that it got stuck in Mr. Crow's throat. Mr.Crow collapsed and struggled to breathe.

Tohru's mother reached him, but now Tohru had a bigger responsibility. He turned around and went into the sea. He expected to be able to walk on water, but the further he went, the more he sank into the water until he was taken by a current and became unconscious.

Chapter eight
The abyss

Tohru opened his eyes. It was underwater. Memories and scenes passed before his eyes. He was a skilled swimmer and had earned the first place in the Olympics. These memories came to Tohru haphazardly. Tohru came to his senses and find himself swimming towards the surface of the water. He reached the top. A memory came to his mind from the time when he was a green genie. He could now walk on water. Tohru ran happily on water towards the end of the sea. He looked down. The little fish was swimming with him in water, looking at him and encouraging him to run faster. He was right. He had never tasted real liberation. He was born a prisoner.

Tohru came up with many other scenes, a cavewoman,

then a Roman soldier, a wanted former Soviet writer who had been forced to change his identity. He had to leave everything behind even his wife and children. Then there was a farmer who didn't age as the years went by and therefor, had witnessed the death of his whole family even his grandchildren with his own eyes. The old man had no one in the world, so he changed his identity again.

Tohru perceived all these, it was very upsetting for him. Tears welled up in his eyes. No matter how far Tohru went, he did not reach the end of the sea. His tears had also dried. He wondered, "What if I reach the end of the sea and I have no tears left...?"

All these thoughts bothered him a lot. Tohru had been walking for a long time. In the beginning he just ran, but when he was relieved that no one could reach him, he slowed down. Maybe it would have been better if Mr. Crow had been still chasing; therefore he would have had run faster and reached the end of the sea sooner. He thought to himself that maybe the big fish sacrificed his life for nothing; but he would have died of the wound anyway. What would happen to his mother? Should he go back to her? Or become a fish himself? Then he looked at the fish's golden fin he had pinned to his clothes. He looked down and saw the baby fish who was having a mixture of longing and despair in his eyes and was staring at Tohru. Tohru could have saved all the fish. He could transform himself as the baby fish's mother in his next state. He just had to forget and leave his life and the people he knew, the earth, and all his attachments behind; the thing he should have done years ago but he was not ready for. Now, after all the different lives he had lived, he realized that the only solution was liberation; otherwise he would have to regret it all his life.

He turned to the sky and muttered under his breath, "Thank you ... for my strength. For all these opportunities over and over again ...."

Tohru looked behind and imagined his mother and said, "I'm sorry but I have to go ...."
Then he turned his face towards the end of the sea and ran fast. Even faster than when Mr. Crow was following him. This time, only the desire for liberation pushed him forward, not fear or coercion or a guilty conscience....
Tohru's cheeks were wet with tears, but this time they were tears of joy.
Tears of liberation...

Chapter nine
The sky

It was reporting on TV that the water crisis was over. Many fishermen had become jobless but were busy taking water to different countries. The conflict over water borders had intensified. The countries that had more water were now more powerful. It was as if the people themselves wanted to create new challenges after solving an old one.The ponds were all out of fish.

Tohru's mother was also looking at the pond in their house, which was being destroyed by workers. She never forgot Tohru, but she understood his great purpose then. She thought to herself that she no longer needed this pond in the middle of the yard. Maybe she could plant a tree in memory of Tohru instead. He had gone to the skies with the fish and was released. The fish were no longer imprisoned in the pond. The sky was now his fish pond.

The End?

Chapter ten

The end of the story from another point of view

A dim light shone in through the window shutters. Sitting at the table was a middle-aged man who, despite his wrinkled face, still had black hair like a crow.

On his desk next to his university degree, there was a board that read:

Dr. Kurosawa PhD in Clinical Psychology....

The man was talking to a woman in her thirties.

Dr. Kurosawa pushed his glasses up his beak-shaped nose and asked: "When exactly did this happen?"

The woman replied, "Well, it happened very slowly. We wanted to have children and we were so overwhelmed that we did not consider other possibilities at all. We even chose a name for our unborn child, and as an instance, I sometimes practiced with my husband and calling him *Yoshiro, my son, come here... .*

The woman had a lump in her throat. Kurosawa gave the woman a glass of water.

The woman had two sips of water and thanked; then continued, "But we could not have any children. This was a big emotional blow to us. At first, I thought it was a blow to me, but I was wrong. After a while, my husband's behavior became childish and he tried to make up for the absence of a child. Honestly speaking, I did not hate it either, and I indulged in this behavior until I realized that we had gone too far, as if he was not willing to stop. I became really desperate; no matter how hard I tried to make him understand that he was an adult, it was of no use. Since the last few days, he has even become delusional and even though there are no fish in our pond, he goes out every night and talks to imaginary fish...."

Mr.Kurosawa asked in surprise, "Why didn›t you come before the situation got so bad?"

The woman answered, "Oh, I did not think it would go so far, I thought it would be right .... But yesterday ... he strangled a cat in water. And then I imprisoned him in the room, I am afraid he would hurt himself.

"Why didn't you bring him?" asked the doctor.

"I fear he might go to the sea because our house is by the sea and he has tried to go there before, but the neighbors helped me take him home. Since then I have never brought him out of the house. I'll appreciate it if you come with me and visit him."

Kurosawa said, "Alright, give me your contact number and address, I will come at the right time."

Then he continued, "Do you have any information about your husband's childhood?"

The woman said, "As far as I know, he did not experience much childhood and most of the time he used to give his father a hand in fishing. His father was a fisherman. As he told me, he did not like it very much."

"That counts a lot." Kurosawa said.

The time for counseling was over. Mr.Kurosawa was guiding the woman out and giving her some advice along the way.

The secretary said, "Dr.Kurosawa, your next appointment has been cancelled.

The woman turned to Dr.Kurosawa and pleaded, "Can you come right now, please?"

The doctor looked at his watch hesitantly and said, "Let's go."

Dr.Kurosawa and the woman arrived at the house.

The woman opened the door and shouted in surprise, "Tohru...!"

Tohru's leg was injured and he had fallen down. Dr.Kurosawa helped him stand up. The woman said to Tohru, "Mr.Kurosawa is here to help you get better and get back to normal."

Tohru looked at Mr.Kurosawa with hatred and said, "You killed my friend. I will kill you, Mr. Crow!"

Tohru kept repeating this sentence.

The woman asked Dr. Kurosawa, " Why does he call you Mr.Crow?"

"It's probably because of the similarity of my last name to crow, and he may have a bad or scary memory of a crow," said Dr.Kurosawa.

Tohru was sitting in the corner of the yard, crying. The woman guided him and the doctor inside the house. Kurosawa turned to the woman and said, "You wait in the hall so I can talk to him alone."

The woman sat in the hall for a few minutes. The question was whether her husband could go back to the old days and no longer be a child. She often had a guilty conscience for her treatment with Tohru. It was really hard to ignore someone who was being lost in front of your eyes, but seemed if there was no other way.

She was in these thoughts that Dr. Kurosawa shouted. The woman got up at once. Tohru was running towards the door. The woman wanted to stop him, but Tohru pushed her away. The door was half open in the yard and Tohru ran out.

The woman hurried to the door and saw Tohru going to the sea. Kurosawa also reached the door and ran faster than the woman and cried, "Wait Tohru! Wait ...Tohruuuuuuuu."

Dr.Kurosawa was approaching Tohru when Tohru threw a stone at his head and rushed to the sea. Dr.Kurosawa's head bled a little, but there was no serious problem.

Dr.Kurosawa and the woman ran towards Tohru, but Tohru threw sand at them. A strong wind was blowing and the sea was stormy.

At the last moment, the woman shouted Tohru's name and begged him not to go into the water. Tohru was a little hesitant, but eventually went into the sea and disappeared a few minutes later.

****

More sorrow was mapped on the woman's face. She was wearing a black dress, but a sense of calmness together with sadness rippled through her eyes. The workers were demolishing the pond.

The woman thought to herself that there was no need
for this pond anymore.
The sky was Tohru's fish pond.

The End

About The Author

Maziar Saffariantoosi was born on September 12, 1995 and is an MS graduate student in Clinical Psychology at Shahid Beheshti University, Tehran, Iran.

He has always been fond of myths, film analysis, reading and writing. His short stories have won numerous awards from the Institute for the Intellectual Development of Children and Young Adults of Iran.

The Sky, My Fish Pond is his first book which he wrote in his twenties.

It is classified as a dark fantasy, with two endings of fantasy and psychology.

Contact the author via:

E-mail: saffarian.m74@yahoo.com

Instagram: maziar.saffarian.psychology

Made in the USA
Las Vegas, NV
11 June 2023

73272023R00033